WITHDRAWN

Charles County Public Library
P.D. Brown Memorial Library
301-645-2864 301-843-7688
www.ccplonline.org

Freddie the Flounder

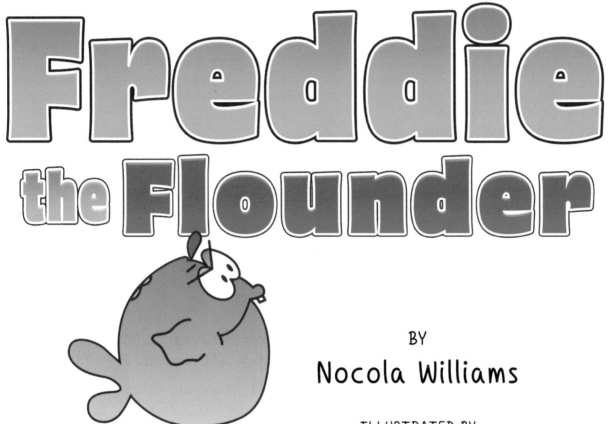

BY

Nocola Williams

ILLUSTRATED BY

Cissy Langley

WITHDRAWN

Freddie the Flounder, Nocola Williams, Cissy Langley

Copyright © 1992

All rights reserved. No part of this publication, or the characters within it, may be reproduced or distributed in any form or by any means without prior written consent from the publisher.

Written by Nocola Williams
Illustrated by Cissy Langley
Edited by Bobbie Hinman
Graphic design by Misty Black Media, LLC and Glaiza Beverly Ganaba

First Edition 2021

Publisher's Cataloging-in-Publication Data

Names: Williams, Nocola, author. | Langley, Cissy, illustrator.
Title: Freddie the flounder / written by Nocola Williams ; illustrated by Cissy Langley.
Description: Leonardtown, MD: The Hip Hop Homestead Press, LLC, 2021. |
Summary: When Freddie the Flounder's parents get swished away by a strong current, he faces his fears and goes on a quest to find them.
Identifiers: LCCN: 2020923874 | ISBN: 978-1-7360696-2-2 (Hardcover) | 978-1-7360696-1-5 (pbk.) | 978-1-7360696-0-8 (ebook)
Subjects: LCSH Fish--Juvenile fiction. | Family--Juvenile fiction. | Marine animals--Juvenile fiction. |Stories in rhyme. | CYAC Fish--Fiction. | Family--Fiction. | Marine animals--Fiction. | BISAC JUVENILE FICTION / General | JUVENILE FICTION / Animals / General | JUVENILE FICTION /Animals / Fish | JUVENILE FICTION / Bedtime & Dreams
Classification: LCC PZ7.1 W55 Fre 2021 | DDC [E]--dc23

For my family, friends, and students...
Be patient, have faith,
don't ever stop chasing your dreams

Special Thanks:
Bobbie Hinman
April Cox
Aurora Alin
Misty Black
Glaiza Beverly Ganaba

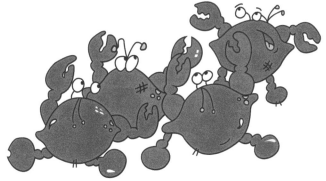

Freddie the flounder
was playing one day,
when a powerful current
swished his parents away.

Freddie thought, "Were they swished
to a strange, unknown place?"
He was scared, you could tell
by the look on his face!

He swam through some coral,
just feeling so sad.
His parents were lost both
his mom and his dad.

Freddie looked between rocks,
even under a plant.
"This sea is too big!" he said,
starting to pant.

Now, how would he find
his mom and his dad?
Not knowing the answer
made Freddie feel sad.

So he sat on a rock
and he started to cry.
Then he had an idea
He'd give it a try!

"I'll just look til I find them!"
he said, feeling brave.
You see, that was the way
he was taught to behave.

The search then began
in the deep, sparkling sea,
with not even one clue where
his parents might be.

As he chose a direction to start his long swim,
ONE big, burly octopus bumped into him.

"Excuse me, have you seen my mom and my dad?"

The octopus answered,
"I have not, little lad."

"I really don't know where your parents could be,
but perhaps you should rest before traveling the sea."

Then kindly he said,
"You can rest in my bed."

But Freddie replied,
"I must scurry instead."

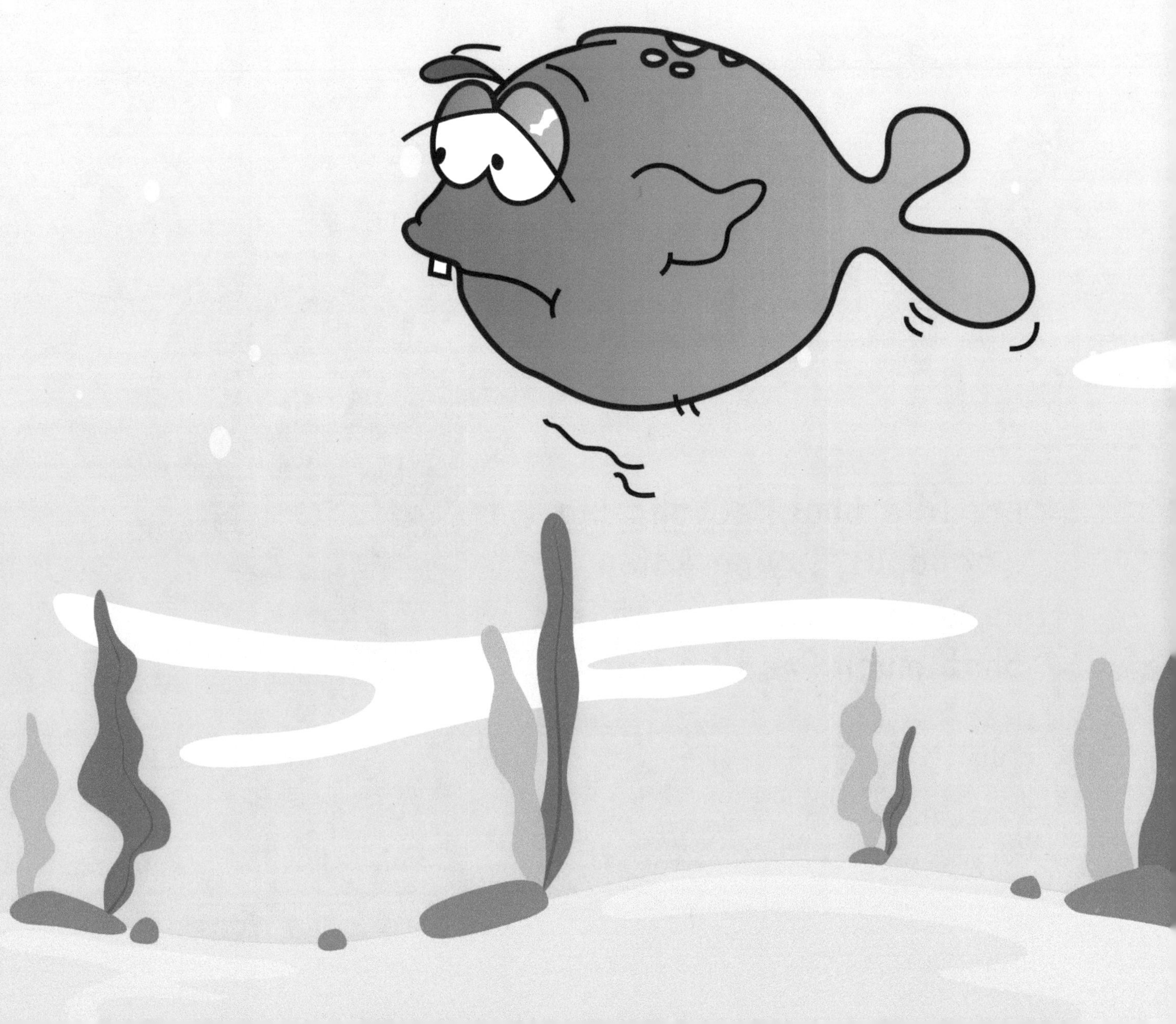

"I'm sorry my stay was really so quick,
but my parents, I know, will be worried quite sick."

Freddie thanked the big
octopus, saying Adieu,
but his plan was important,
that much Freddie knew.

He swam a bit longer
and what did he spy?

There were **TWO** playful dolphins
doing flips in the sky.

He swam up to a dolphin,
the biggest by far.
"Have you seen my parents?
Do you know where they are?"

"No, no, no, no, no...no flounders in sight,
but it's getting so late.
How about spending the night?"

Freddie said, "I can't stay.
See, I really must hurry.
I know that my parents
are so full of worry."

Freddie looked inside caves
and he looked on the ground.
But it seemed that his parents
were nowhere around.

Then he saw **THREE** young clams
playing catch with a pearl.
They said, "Hello, flounder,
want to give it a whirl?"

"Not now," Freddie said.
"There is no time for play.
I can't find my parents.
They were both swished away."

As he swam past the clams at such a fast pace,
it was almost as if he were running a race.

Freddie then met a family of crabs—
there were **FOUR**,
and he asked if his parents
had been seen near the shore.

"Um—no," was the answer
each one of them said.
"But we can't help you now.
We are going to bed."

Poor Freddie was scared
and was clearly upset,
but he couldn't give up...
no, he couldn't...not yet.

When FIVE bright sea turtles swam lazily by,
Freddie thought, "I should ask them.
It won't hurt to try."

He went up to the turtles
and burst into tears.
"Don't cry, little fish," they said.
"What are your fears?"

Freddie answered, with tears streaming down his sad face
"I have looked for my parents all over the place."

It seems that they've vanished
right out of the sea.
Can you help? Do you know
where my parents could be?"

"Can't say that we've seen them in this neighborhood, but you look very tired and that's just not good."

"You should rest for a while and start looking tomorrow."

Freddie felt oh, so sad as his heart filled with sorrow.

Feeling tired and sleepy, he called it a night,
then he lay on a rock and he shut his eyes tight.
He tossed and he turned, and he turned and he tossed.
Freddie felt so alone and now he, too, was lost.

He let out a whimper, and then a loud scream,
when he woke up to find it had all been a

He sat up in bed and realized then...
that his scary adventure had come to an end.

The End

COMING SOON!

Freddie the Flounder

Goes to School!

About the Author:

Nocola Williams has an EdD in Teacher Leadership and loves sharing the joy of learning with her favorite people—her students. Her passion for reading has spanned her entire life and is one of the reasons she became an elementary school teacher. Nocola's favorite part of teaching is watching her students get whisked away into their own imaginations as she reads aloud to them. Nocola and her husband have two adult children and a new grandson who is the greatest gift her family has ever received.

About the Illustrator:

Cissy Langley's love of art began when she was very young. She attended the Maryland Institute of Art, where she later met her husband. After a colleague sent one of her drawings to a local newspaper, the rest, as they say, is history. Cissy has been sharing her love of art ever since. She specializes in caricatures and mixed media designs made from felt, canvas and plastic. Her work can be seen at several Maryland art galleries. Cissy and her husband have one adult son and two grandsons.

Follow Freddie's journey!

www.thehiphophomestead.com

CPSIA information can be obtained
at www.ICGtesting.com
Printed in the USA
BVHW061400300421
605595BV00001B/3